Black All Around!

by Patricia Hubbell

illustrated by Don Tate

LEE & LOW BOOKS Inc.
New York

Text copyright © 2003 by Patricia Hubbell
Illustrations copyright © 2003 by Don Tate

LEE & LOW BOOKS Inc., 95 Madison Avenue, New York, NY 10016
www.leeandlow.com

The artist would like to acknowledge the Moore family, who served as
models for the paintings in this book: Durwood Sr., Lisa, Gabrielle and
D.J. (Durwood Jr.).

Manufactured in China

Book design by David Neuhaus/NeuStudio
Book production by The Kids at Our House

The text is set in 17 point Chianti Bold
The illustrations are rendered in acrylic paint on paper

10 9 8 7 6 5 4 3 2
First Edition

Library of Congress Cataloging-in-Publication Data
Hubbell, Patricia.
Black all around! / by Patricia Hubbell ; illustrated by Don
Tate.— 1st ed.
p. cm.
Summary: An African American girl contemplates the many
wonderful black things around her, from the inside of a pocket,
where surprises hide, to the cozy night where there is no light.
ISBN 1-58430-048-5
[1. Black—Fiction. 2. African Americans—Fiction. 3. Stories
in rhyme.] I. Tate, Don, ill. II. Title.
PZ8.3.H848 Bl 2003   [E]—dc21   2002067125

For my book-loving, librarian Aunt,
Dorothy Goodsell Hubbell
—P.H.

For Autumn, Jheris and Kolby Tate.
"Dad loves you!"
—D.T.

Look high,
look low,
look everywhere . . .
The wonderful color black is there!

Sleek and jazzy,
warm and cozy.
Beautiful black,
black all around . . .

The inside of a pocket
where surprises hide.

A nighttime lake
where fishes glide.

mole hole

letters

limousine

The letters that live
on each page of a book.
The hole in the ground
that's a little mole's nook.
The gleaming paint on a limousine.
The braided hair of a stately queen.

A big workhorse.
Some cats, of course.
Glossy beetles.
Busy ants.
The clothes men wear to a fancy dance.

The crack in a wall
where a chipmunk scoots.
A firefighter's boots.
The gentle eyes of a fawn and a doe.
A long, long tunnel where a train goes slow.

Beautiful black,
black all around . . .
Like the back of a dream of stars and moon
that floats through your head on an afternoon
when you take a nap in a big old chair.

Velvet soft.
Satin sleek.
Daddy's arm.
Momma's cheek.

The headlines in the daily news.
Patent leather party shoes.
Clarinets and piano keys.
The fuzzy stripes on bumblebees.
A polished stone.
A licorice twist.

Tall trunks of trees in morning mist.

Car tracks that curve
through fresh new snow
and make you wonder
where they go.

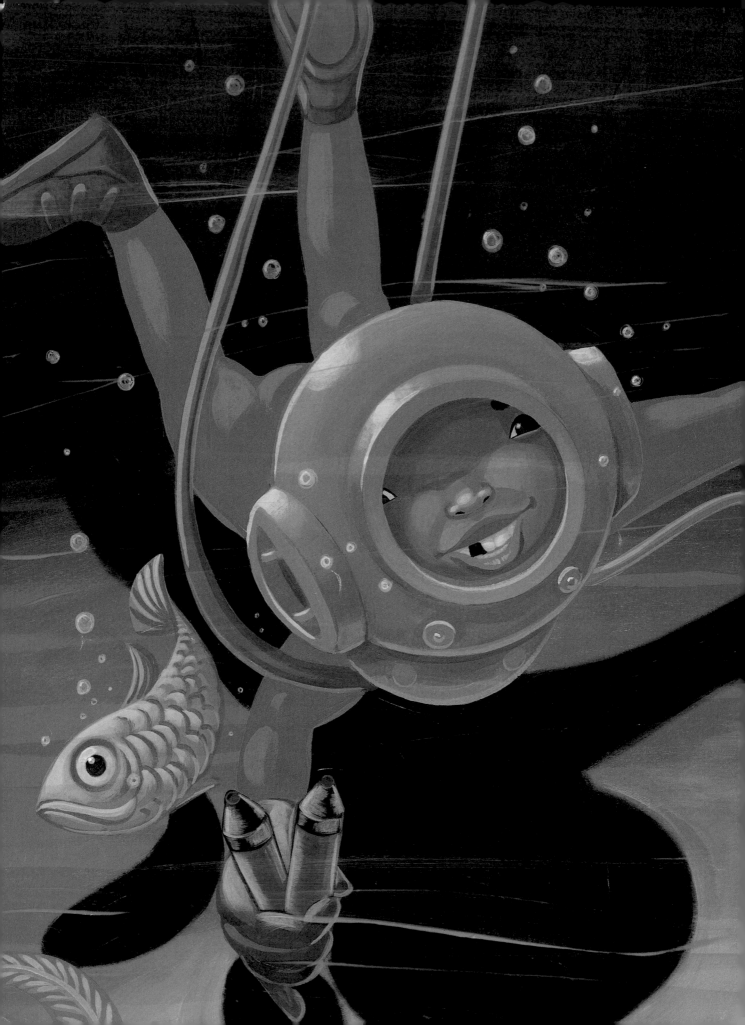

Crayons.
Crickets.
The bottom of the sea.
The empty place where a tooth should be.

A ladybug's spots.
A clown's polka dots.
The rich, damp dirt in a flowerpot.

Labrador retrievers.
   Lively poodles.
      Inky squiggles and splotches and doodles.

Some chickens, bunnies,
cows, and goats.
The closet where we store
our winter coats.

The cozy night
when there is no light,
when the dark breathes deep
and you drift to sleep . . .

dreaming your dream
of beautiful black,
black all around.